In the Beak of a Duck

By Alan Gettis

Illustrated by Kyle Wade

GOODMAN BECK PUBLISHING

In the Beak of a Duck
Copyright 2008 by Alan Gettis

ISBN: 978-0-97987-550-2
Library of Congress Control Number: 2008900962

Goodman Beck Publishing
P.O. Box 253
Norwood, NJ 07648-2428
www.goodmanbeck.com

10 9 8 7 6 5 4 3 2 1

FIRST EDITION

In memory of my dad, who taught me everything I know about being silly. And for my mom, who taught me so many things throughout her life.

—Alan Gettis

And for Tim Milhorn, a great teacher and inspiration.

—Kyle Wade

Table of Contents

Acknowledgements

My daughter Jenna is a very gifted graphic designer.
She played a very significant role in the artistic design of
this book, and I am greatly appreciative of that. Kyle Wade
believed in this project from day one, and his wonderful
illustrations are perfect compliments to the poems.

I began to write silly poems after reading the brilliant and
zany Shel Silverstein and the amazing Dr. Seuss. I owe them
a great debt of gratitude. The word silly is of Middle English
origin (seli, silli) and means blessed, innocent and happy.
The silly poems in this book are for children and grown-ups.

I like nonsense - it wakes up the brain cells. Fantasy is a
necessary ingredient in living. It's a way of looking at life
through the wrong end of a telescope... and that enables you
to laugh at all of life's realities.

—Dr. Seuss

Put Something In

Draw a crazy picture,
Write a nutty poem,
Sing a mumble-grumble song,
Whistle through your comb.
Do a loony-goony dance
'Cross the kitchen floor,
Put something silly in the world
That ain't been there before.

—Shel Silverstein

Our Conversation

He said, "Did too."
I said, "Did not!"

He said, "Did too."
I said, "Did not!"

He said, "DID TOO!"
I said, "DID NOT!"

Other than that,
We didn't say a lot.

My Uncle's Beard

My uncle's beard
Is so long,
It actually hits the floor.

One time,
When he came visiting,
It got stuck in the door.

At Christmas time
It's wonderful,
We decorate it like a tree.

With ornaments, and tinsel,
And lights for
Everyone to see.

And I know
It must sound funny,
And you may think it's weird,

That the gifts
On Christmas morning
Go beneath my uncle's beard!

A Cold Day in July

It's freezing cold and windy,
The snow is piling high.
It's all quite unexpected,
This is the middle of July.

I thought I would be swimming,
Basking in the sun.
Dashing, thrashing, splashing, and
Having lots of fun.

But instead we're throwing snowballs,
One just smacked me in the eye.
And that's the end of this poem,
Because I'm going to cry.

Surprise

I shaved my beard,
And what I found
Really made me grin.

I had two cheeks,
A nose, and mouth,
But I didn't have a chin.

Donut Man

He couldn't leap tall buildings,
He weighed about 1000 pounds.
"Donut Man" was immeasurable,
And made repulsive burping sounds.

He wasn't strong like "Superman,"
He couldn't win a fight,
But he could eat ten donuts
In a single bite.

Your hero may be "Spiderman,"
Who's the opposite of a "wimp."
But I'll take jumbo "Donut Man"
Who's shaped just like a blimp.

He wasn't fast, he wasn't smart,
He never saved a person.
But if there weren't any donuts,
Wow, you'd hear him cursin'.

Donuts for breakfast,
For lunch, and for dinner.
When it comes to superheroes,
"Donut Man's" the winner!

Woof

My doctor was so busy
So I went to see the vet.
She examined me, and rubbed my belly,
As if I were a pet.

She said, "Sit! Speak!
And now roll over."
Then, to my surprise,
She said, "Atta boy, Rover!"

The doctors told my mother,
"No ifs, or ands, not even a but.
There's no doubt about it,
You have a very healthy mutt!"

My Barber

My barber said,
"Would you like a haircut?"
I replied, "I would."

So he cut one hair,
Then said, "You're finished
And you're looking good!"

Because he only
Cut one hair,
I thought he might be lazy.

But since the hair he cut
Was on my arm,
I decided he must be crazy.

Fat Cat

That spotted old cat
Grew so fat,
He couldn't even say, "Meow."

He'd say, "Moo,
What's wrong with me?
I'm a cat. I'm not a cow."

He started giving milk,
Gave up cat toys,
And walked slowly through the mud.

He stopped eating mice,
He grazed on grass,
And then, he'd chew his cud.

Too bad he wasn't a cow,
Because as a cat,
He was a dud!

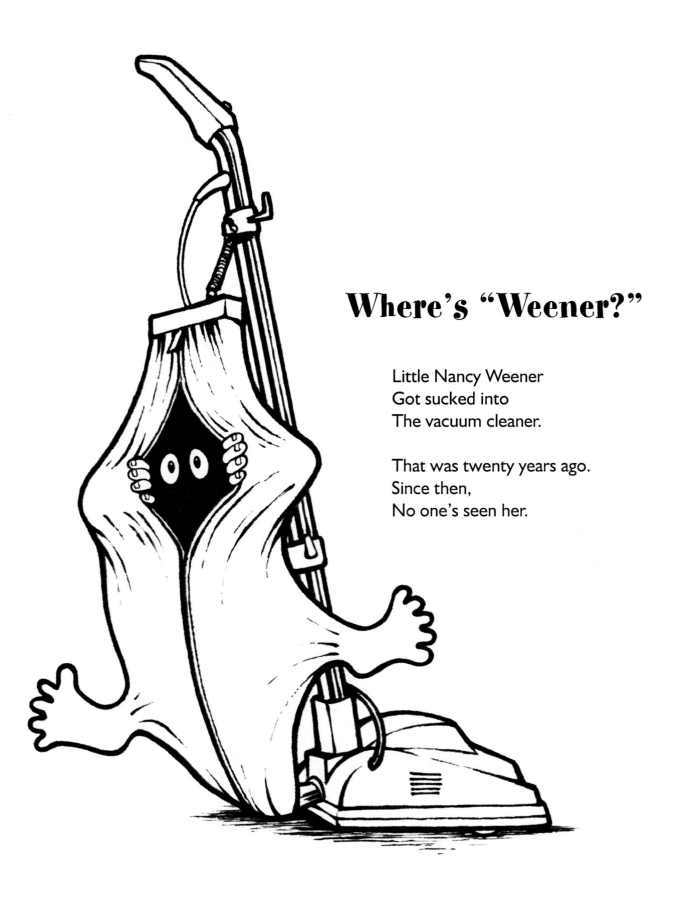

Where's "Weener?"

Little Nancy Weener
Got sucked into
The vacuum cleaner.

That was twenty years ago.
Since then,
No one's seen her.

That's Not Nice

I feel cruel,
I feel guilty.

I feel evil,
I feel sick.

I just bit
Off the head

Of a yellow
Marshmallow chick.

Show & Tell

Mr. William Tell
Took his arrow and his bow,
And said, "Down in history
I'm sure I'll go.

I'll shoot an apple off
The head of a boy.
The whole wide world
Will shout with joy."

Unfortunately, he missed.
Ooooooooops! Oh gee...
Now there's an apple where
The boy's head ought to be!

Ouch

There may be a pebble
In my shoe,
And I'm not sure
What I should do.

It hurts when I walk,
It hurts when I run,
It hurts when I hop and skip.
It hurts when I dance,
It hurts when I prance,
It hurts when I do a back flip.

I could take off my sneaker,
I could take off my sock.
I know I would discover
A very little rock.

But I'm so very lazy,
I'll walk around in pain.
So you'll just have to listen
While I constantly complain.

Can I Take Your Temperature?

I hate thermometers,
Don't you?

They make me choke,
They don't taste good,

And they turn me blue!

Disgusting & Awful

I've never, ever
Seen it yet,
But I know that I can,
I'd be willing to bet.

If I get up quickly
In the middle of the night,
And hop out of the bed
And turn on the light,

I'll see it, I know.
So smelly and gross,
Disgusting and awful
With hundreds of toes.

And after that
It can never be said,
That I didn't see
The "foot of the bed."

Hmmmmm

The train was flying
To Kalamazoo,
The plane choo-chooing
To Timbuktu.

The car floated smoothly
On Beaver Dam,
The boat got caught
In a traffic jam.

The snowmobile
Won't go on snow.
The go-cart,
Well, it just won't go.

The sled slides uphill,
But not down.
Helicopters are riding
In the town.

I thought about taking
My bike for a ride,
But something tells me
To just stay inside.

Horace

My parents hid the Easter eggs
Throughout the entire house.
They forgot about "Horace"
The 327 pound Easter egg eating mouse.

He found all the striped ones,
The orange ones, the blue.
The purple, the yellow, green, and red,
And the eggs with rainbows too.

We hunted for those Easter eggs,
But none were to be found.
Only heaps of eggshells,
Piled on the ground.

So the next time it is Easter,
And eggs are hidden in your house,
Beware of that beast "Horace"
The 349 pound Easter egg eating mouse!

Delicious

"I can touch my tongue
To my nose," I said
To a boy named Matt.

He said, "If you can touch
Your tongue to your nose,
I will eat my hat."

So I did it while
The other kids yelled,
"Hey, Matt, look at that!"

And Matt got ketchup,
Mustard, and relish, and
Quickly ate his hat.

Minnie

Minnie was so skinny,
When she turned sideways,
She'd disappear.

Everyone would look for her,
"Did you see Minnie?
Where, oh where?"

Skinny Minnie
Was so upset,
Because she was so thin.

She said, "Bring me a pie,"
And she ate it all,
Including the pie tin.

For three straight years
She ate pies
Until it truly changed her size.

There is no more Skinny Minnie,
Now she's known as
"Thunder Thighs!"

Mr. Baxter

I don't feel well,
I'm turning blue,
I'm eating lunch
And can hardly chew.

Milk is spilling down my chin,
Going east, west, north, and south.
Mr. Baxter says to me,
"Hey, you have a hole in your mouth!"

I see a hole in my pants,
And there's a hole in my sweater...
But I don't see a hole in my mouth,

So I guess that I'm getting better.

Olives & Orangutans

The elephant lost his trunk,
It was nowhere around.
He didn't know what to do,
So he checked the lost & found.

There were olives & orangutans,
Lots of socks, and old school lunches,
Buttons, hats, and vampire fangs,
And umbrellas by the bunches.

A pirate sword,
An old tin soldier,
One CD player,
And a massive boulder.

So, if you see an elephant
With vampire fangs and a pirate sword,
He probably will be missing his trunk...
But he certainly won't be bored!

Bowling is Fun

I went bowling,
First time ever.
I forgot to let go of the ball.

I slid until
I reached the pins,
That were all standing tall.

I kicked as many as I could,
And shoved them
With my free hand.

I was screaming
As I knocked them over.
It sounded like a band.

And when the dust had settled,
The announcer
Grabbed the mike,

And told the entire bowling alley
I had just
Gotten a strike.

BURRP

Zoo

I heard that cow say, "Oink"
I heard that pig say, "Moo."
The owl roared, the lion soared,
The bear said, "Cock-a-doodle-doo!"

The tiger chirped,
The giraffe just burped,
And the zebra sung, "Cuckoo."

The elephant snored,
The baby lamb roared,
It was the strangest zoo!!!

No Big Deal

I lost my belly button
And I was quite distressed,
But it only seemed to matter
When I got undressed.

The Incredible Time Machine

When I grow up
What would I like to be?
That's what grown-ups
Are always askin' me.

If I could go into the future,
See what's ahead of me,
Maybe then I would know
Just what I want to be.

So I traveled 50 years ahead
In an incredible time machine,
And now let me tell you
Exactly what I seen.

I was old, and bald, and wrinkly,
A hearing aid in my left ear.
My belly was growing by the moment,
And I had a big, fat rear.

I was busy paying mortgages,
Taxes and other bills.
I was worried about my health,
And took lots of medicine pills.

Well, now I know what I want to be,
And it may sound wild...
But more than anything, when I grow up,
I'd like to be a child!

Yuk!

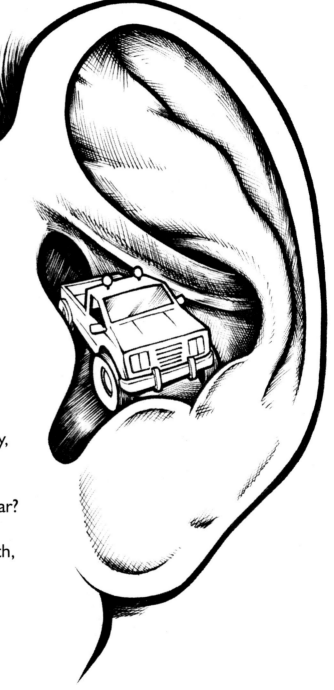

Gook, grease and slime,
A dead ant, hair, and garden hose.
That will be the final time
I ever look into my nose.

Three cavities, some popcorn,
And stains from north to south.
That'll be the very last time
I look into my mouth.

A small toy truck that's rusted out
Sits well within one ear.
The other one's filled with Silly Putty,
And, what is that? Oh dear!

Is it any wonder that I can hardly hear?

So, excuse me while I brush my teeth,
Clean my ears, and blow my nose.
In a minute I'll be sparkling clean,
And smelling like a rose.

Too Big for the Tub

I had a friendly lizard.
He was cute, but grew and grew.
Now, he's over eleven feet tall,
And I don't know what to do.

We put him in the yard,
'Cause he's too big for the tub,
And he ate three of my fingers
Instead of his lizard grub.

cute
friendly
Lizard
for Sale

We hired a guard to watch him,
Put out a pail of fingers for food.
We hoped that he'd be well behaved,
That he never would be rude.

When he ate the fingers and the guard,
And he even ate the pail,
We put up a sign that read,
"Cute Friendly Lizard, For Sale."

Father's Day

I only have one shoe,
And I don't know what to do.

If I put it on my left foot,
My right foot will be mad.

If I put it on my right foot,
My left foot will be sad.

I could put it in the garbage,
But that would be so bad.

Instead I'm going to wrap it up,
And give it to my dad.

Vacation

Pancakes for breakfast
With syrup and butter.
Miniature golf
With a new putter.

Pails, and shovels,
And sand on the beach.
Sunny blue skies,
Ocean waves I can reach.

CD's, and movies,
"Wiffleball" too.
"Monopoly," "Candyland,"
And a long game of "Clue."

Gee, it's only 2 o'clock...
Now, what can we do?

Zeke

He's a freak,
And a meek geek
With a huge beak,

And he's weak
And a sneak,
And boy, does he
reek...

My best friend Zeke.

Mmm, Mmm Good

My teacher said I should eat better,
That I'd be smarter in school.
I told him that I would try to,
'Cause I did not want to be a fool.

Next morning, I took fish out of our tank,
And spiced them with pepper and salt.
As part of that wonderful breakfast,
I included a chocolate malt.

At school, I told my teacher
All about my morning feast.
He yelled, "Never eat breakfast again!"
And called me a little beast.

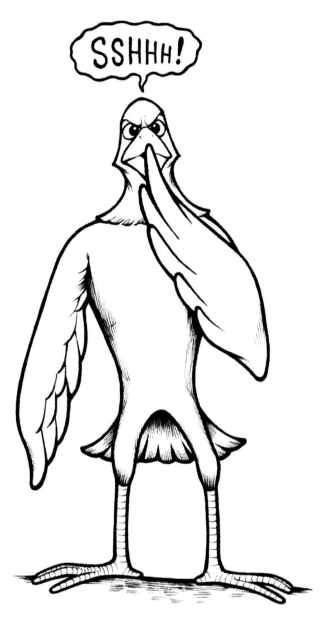

Not a Word

I know this game, I've played it
Several times before.
The first one who talks loses,
So I won't say no more.

I won't say a word,
Not a sound from me.
I'll be quiet as a bird,
As silent as can be.

It's been sixteen hours now...
I'm hungry, tired, and cranky.
I'm feeling sick, my nose is running,
And I don't have a hanky.

I don't want to play this stupid game!
It really is quite boring...
And for fifteen hours now,
I've listened to your snoring.

So, not a word was spoken,
But of this I'll say no more.
Excuse me while I silently
Walk right out the door.

A Camel Without a Hump

There was once a kangaroo
Without a pouch,
And a camel
Without a hump.

A zebra without
Black and white stripes,
A gas station
Without a pump.

There was once a sky
Without stars, sun, or moon.
There once was a year
Without any June.

If something important
Was missing in you,
How would you be,
And what would you do?

Each day PLEASE
Be thankful,
You have
All that you do.

The Blizzard of 2003

How old to you have to be
To remember the blizzard of 2003?

Where cars ran amuck,
And even tow trucks got stuck.
We were all out of luck
In the blizzard of 2003.

So, it was something to see,
That blizzard of 2003.
It was quite a fright
Through day and through night.

Nothin' but white,
The blizzard of 2003.

Could we ever dig out
From three feet of snow?
Or was it more like
Four feet, or five?

It was touch and go,
And we had our doubts,
Would we ever
Get out alive?

When I think of that blizzard
of 2003,
I find that I still quiver.

And the most horrible thing
About the blizzard,
Was that the pizza place
Wouldn't deliver.

Mixed Up Michael

Michael mixed up
His hands and his feet.
He put on his socks for mittens,
And used his toes to eat.

And if that wasn't odd enough,
You know what he did with his toes?
It wasn't a pretty picture,
When Michael picked his nose.

Love in Bloom?

She said I'm uglier
Than a frog,

Stinkier
Than a hog,

And dumber
Than a log.

I think she likes me...
Don't you?

I'll Trade You

Jennifer lived in Arizona.
It was warm and sunny every day.
Billy lived in North Dakota,
Icy cold in every way.

Jennifer longed to make a snowman,
Use a carrot for his nose.
Billy wished for hotter weather,
To warm his icy toes.

Jen prayed for a white Christmas,
For snowball fights and sledding.
Billy prayed for clear blue skies,
And lots of warm, warm bedding.

Jen was surprised on Christmas morning,
A large box had come from Billy.
He had sent her winter,
And though that sounds quite silly,

She skied and she threw snowballs,
Built a snowman and ice-skated.
While Billy sat quietly
By his mailbox, and waited.

Sure enough, a huge box came,
Jen hadn't let him down.
A smile formed across his face,
And took away the frown.

She sent Arizona sun and heat,
And he played, and swam, and ran.
And during that icy North Dakota winter,
Billy had a tan!

The Jungle

My mom wasn't home to tuck me in.
I had a hard time getting to sleep.
I dreamed I was riding in a jungle,
Sitting in an open Jeep.

The Jeep didn't have a steering wheel,
And it was going toward a tree.
It was all so very scary,
I was frightened as can be.

And to make it
Even worse,
Wild tigers were
After me.

And then, suddenly it happened,
But not what you'd expect,
The wild tigers never got me,
The Jeep was never wrecked.

I flew away so gently,
And landed in my bed.
It was morning, and it felt so good,
"Wake up," my mother said.

Nice Try, Mom

Mom said, "If you're good
You can have collard greens
And brussel sprouts."

"I know you would
Really enjoy them.
Of this, I don't have any doubts."

So I was good
And she gave me the veggies
Yuk! It must have been a joke!

I said, "Mom, next time I'm good,
How about french-fries
And a Coke?"

Nail Biting Sue

Suzie bites her nails.
Chews 'em and swallows 'em too.
She knows it's a bad habit,
She's known as Nail Biting Sue.

When it comes to nail biting,
She not only bites her own,
She'll chew and swallow
Ryan's nails, and her best friend Joan.

When her friends' nails are all gone,
She'll even start on strangers,
She'll bite and swallow their nails too,
Nothing's gonna change her.

It's hard for me to explain,
I hope that I don't stammer,
Uh, but the kind of nails Suzie chews
Are the kind that you hit with a hammer.

She's got sharp nails in her stomach,
And nails in her lung,
Nails in her kidney,
And nails stuck in her tongue.

They've punctured all her organs,
Scratched her bones, and tore her muscles.
They've damaged her esophagus,
And her red corpuscles.

They're sticking out her body,
And tearing all her clothes.
She's got a bunch coming out her back,
And three coming out her nose.

So, if you have a bad habit,
And you don't know what to do,
Say, "Hey, well things could be worse.
I could be Nail Biting Sue".

(never, ever put nails in your mouth)

45

Play Ball

My dad hit a ball
So high in the air,
We thought it would never come
down.

It was our
One and only ball,
So we just waited around.

It hit a bunch of ducks,
As they glided
Through the sky.

One of them
Fell down,
And hit me in the eye.

And there it was
In the beak
Of a duck,

The ball
That dad hit,
And it was stuck.

So, our ballgame was over,
We were out of luck.
Darn that beak,
And Darn that duck!

My Grampa

Grampa finds dimes
In my ears.
Once he found
A quarter!

Twice he cured
My hiccups
By giving me
Sugar-water.

He tells me stories,
He tells me jokes,
He hardly ever says "No."

He's always glad
To see me.
I like the Grampa-Show!

It's Raining Again

It's raining again, it's raining again,
For the 40th day in a row.
Everything's floating, including our house,
There's no place that I want to go.

Dad yells to get the oars,
Mom says to get my coat.
And sure enough it's happening,
We're going to school in a boat.

How Rude

A squirrel came down our chimney
And ended up on our living room floor.

My mom said, "That's not very nice,
Next time, use the door!"

The Bathroom

I have to go
To the bathroom.
I have to go very bad.

If I don't get
To a bathroom,
I'm going to be very sad.

I'm not sure that
I can hold it,
It's such a terrible strain.

I can't think
Of anything else,
Except the horrible pain.

I no longer
Need a bathroom,
Now, I'm ready to dance.

Now, I'm ready for travel
To England,
Denmark, or France.

Just excuse me
For a minute,
I have to change my pants!

Ah Choo!!!

I sneezed in the library.
The librarian said,
"God bless you."

Again I sneezed,
"Gesundheit," she said.
I sneezed, "Achooo, achooo."

She said, "Enough's enough!
You'll have to be
More quiet."

I sneezed
Seventeen more times,
It sounded like a riot.

She warned me
Not to sneeze again,
She said she'd call a cop.

I tried, and tried,
I tried so hard,
But I couldn't stop.

Tables turned over
And books went flying.
The sneezing stopped,
And I'm not lying.

The librarian
Was under a pile of books,
Battered, bruised and crying.

French Fries

How do I know
Where anything's from,
If french-fries aren't from France?

Will human beings
Run around naked,
While dogs and cats wear pants?

If Buffalo-Wings
Aren't from buffaloes...
Then it seems that anything goes.

Maybe we'll have schools
All over the moon,
And be riding on UFO's.

How do I know
What anything means,
If a hamburger isn't from ham?

How do I know
What "this" or "that" is,
And how do I know
Who I am?

If grapefruits
Aren't from grapes,
What is it that I really know?

Are hotdogs from dogs?
Is anything real?
Or is it a "make-believe-show?"

I guess I'm not sure
Of this or of that.
Is that a donkey,
Or a cat in a hat?

Is this
Really this?
And is that
Really that?

Life could be so simple,
I'd celebrate and dance,
If only those french-fries
Simply came from France.

Home Sweet Home

There was an old woman
Who lived in a shoe.
She got caught in the laces,
And turned black and blue.

So she moved to a doghouse
In the far end of town.
But, it was so muddy
That she turned to dark brown.

So she moved to an igloo
With just snow in her sight.
And by the end of winter,
She had turned white.

Then she moved to Canaryville.
Everyone said "Chirp" and "Hello!"
But by the end of the spring,
She was turning yellow.

So she moved to a lemonade stand,
And oh, did she drink.
By the end of the summer,
She was nothing but pink.

Wherever she went,
She kept turning colors,
Like orange, and purple, and red.

Finally, she just went
Back to her shoe,
And solved the problem by using her head.

She simply removed
All the shoe laces,
And quickly fell asleep in her bed.

Upcreek Without a Paddle

I don't feel quite myself today.
But if I'm not me,
Who am I?

I feel a bit peculiar,
Yet I'm not sure
How or why?

It's like I'm riding backwards
In the saddle, not knowing
If I'm coming or going.

Like being upcreek
Without a paddle,
So I couldn't do any rowing.

Something's missing,
But I don't know what.
It's like a baby's crib without a rattle.

It's like a civil war
Without a battle,
Like a dairy farm without cattle.

I just don't feel myself today,
I feel like
Something is gone.

Oops, I just figured it out...
I forgot to put my pants on.

Nelly

I have a friend
And his name is "Nelly."

A delicatessen
Is known as a deli.
He ate too much there
And got a big belly.

And then he had jam,
Boy was it smelly.
Now you know all
About my friend,

Smelly-Deli-Jelly-Belly Nelly.

The Basement

I'm afraid to go down
To the basement by myself.
I'm afraid of what I'll see.

Slimy lizards,
And headless people,
And a gargantuan bumblebee.

I know they're all hiding,
Lurking about...
Just waiting for me,
And then they'll come out.

There'll be evil witches
With skeleton bones,
And horrible monsters
Making terrible groans.

Mom and dad think I'm silly
To have all these fears,
They say that it's all
In my head.

They'd be very happy
If I walked down those stairs...
But I know if I did,
I'd be dead!

Mudville

It had rained all week,
It was early spring,
And there was mud all over the place.

A boy asked me to play with him,
He had mud
All over his face.

He said, "We can make mud sandwiches,
And we can make mud pies.
We can spit mud back and forth
Into each other's eyes."

Mud in our ears,
Mud up our noses,
Mud on our tongues,
Mud between our toes'es.

Mud for breakfast,
Lunch, and dinner.
Mud for the loser, and
Mud for the winner.

We wouldn't have mothers.
Instead we'd have "mudders."
We'd be the muddlers,
From muddy Mudville.

We'd play with mud cats,
Mudfish, and mud hens.
And we'd each take
A vita mud pill.

There'd be mud turtles,
Mud snakes, and our twenty mud fingers.
We would be known
As famous mudslingers.

I answered, "It's clear as mud!
I can see it all now.
But there's one little thing you should know...

I really hate baths,
So I'm staying clean,
And I guess that I should just go."

Jimmy McCall

Jimmy McCall
Was twelve feet tall.
You could say
He was a giant.

He never listened to anyone,
In fact,
He was defiant.

He could not stand
Inside his house,
His head would hit the ceiling.

Once, he forgot
And smashed his head.
Bang! It sent him reeling.

Being he was twelve feet tall,
He took a nasty giant-sized fall.
And that was the end of Jimmy McCall.

One-Eyed Purple People Eater

What exactly is a
One-eyed purple people eater?

Is it someone with one eye,
That eats purple people?

Or is it someone with one eye,
Who is purple, and eats people?

Or, is it a creature that eats
One-eyed purple people?

Even though I don't know
Exactly what it is,
I know it's more scary
Than fun...

So, if I ever
See it coming,
The first thing I'll do is
RUUUUUUUUUUUUN!!!

Wishes Can Come True

I wish I had a motor,
I wish I had some wings.
It would be a lot of fun
If I had a dog that sings.

But I don't have a motor,
And I don't have any wings,
And I don't even have a dog,
But I have a lot of things.

Like a great imagination,
And that is why I say,
It's time for me to go outside
And jump, and run, and play.

So please turn on my motor,
And activate my wings,
And listen to my doggie
As he speaks, and rhymes, and sings.

Mr. Miller

Mr. Miller
Had a clock for a face.
His eyes were at "3" and "9."

His chin was at "6,"
His forehead at "12,"
It really was quite divine.

He never was early,
He never was late.
He was always right on time.

He never spoke,
He just tick-ticked.
And on the hour he'd chime.

Mr. Miller grew old,
His clock face rusted.
One day he fell,
And his clock face busted.

Poor old Mr. Miller,
It was quite a terrible shock.
He gave his final tick-tock-tick,
And his final tock-tick-tock.

So don't be early,
And don't be late,
But always be on time.

That's the end
Of Mr. Miller,
And this very timely rhyme.

Big Deal

My puppy sits
And rolls over,
Then he gets a treat.

My baby sister
Says, "Mama."
People think that's neat.

I can sit,
And roll over,
And I can say, "Mama" too.

But whenever I do these things,
People say, "Big deal," and
"So what else can you do?"

So, I'm beginning to think
Maybe, yeah,
Just maybe...

Sometimes, I would rather be
A puppy
Or a baby.

Honesty

The dog
Ate my homework,
That may sound
Like a lame excuse.

But it's better
Than last week's story,
When it was
Eaten by a moose.

Flying High

If I fell from the top
Of the Empire State Building,

I'd soar like an eagle,
I'd circle like a buzzard,

I'd hoot-hoot like an owl,
I'd glide like a gull,

I'd chirp like a robin,
I'd yell, "Polly wants a cracker!"

I'd honk like a goose,
I'd...

SPLAT!!!

The End

Pass the Jelly

I'm afraid, if I eat a turkey,
I will start to gobble.
I'm afraid if I eat a three-legged chicken,
I will start to hobble.

If I eat a pork chop,
Will I become a pig?
If I eat a beaver,
Will all I do is dig?

If I eat a steak,
I'm scared I'll start to moo.
I'm afraid, if I eat animals,
I'll wind up in a zoo.

So, all I eat is jelly,
Morning, noon, and night.
And they call me "Jelly-Belly,"
And I'm not a pretty sight!

Alice's Room

Alice had the messiest room
In the whole wide universe,
Including Saturn, Istanbul,
Mars, and all the Earth.

No one knew
Just what to do
With that unbelievably messy room.

So they got a bomb,
And that was it.
BOOOOOOOOOOOOM!!!

Keep Your Head

Al E. Gator
Met Frank N. Stein.
They haunted and taunted,
And had a good time.

'Til Mr. Gator
Bit off Mr. Stein's head,
And swallowed it whole,
But Frank was not dead.

He crushed Al E. Gator
With one mighty smack,
Reached into his stomach
And took his head back.

He carries it with him
Wherever he goes,
He dresses it up
In buttons and bows.

He sometimes keeps it
In a burlap sack.
Once he stuffed it
In a fanny pack.

He takes it for a haircut,
He takes it for a shave,
And if and when he ever dies,
He'll take it to his grave.

So, although he's really headless,
He hasn't lost his head.
He puts it on a separate pillow
When he goes to bed.

So take a lesson
From Frank N. Stein,
Whether you have one head,
Or even eight or nine.

Treat your head well
And always keep it in sight,
Because without your head,
You won't know wrong from right.

Farkle

Once, I had a pet fly,
And I named him "Farkle."
He was very special,
You should have seen him sparkle.

He'd sit upon my fingertip,
And I'd tell him stories.
He loved to watch cartoons with me,
And smell the morning glories.

I taught him tricks,
I told him news.
He even learned
To shine my shoes.

I fed him lots of rice and beans,
He liked them with ketchup and spice.
He was only my pet for a few weeks,
But ah, it was so nice.

I still miss Farkle, my pet fly,
And I think I always will.
Sometimes, I still look for him
Upon the windowsill.

Of Brains & Wits

Mr. and Mrs. Brain
Had two children,
And they named them
"Bird" and "Lame."

If you think
Those names are funny,
Well, the parents
Are to blame.

Mr. and Mrs. Wit
Had two kids,
And they named them
"Nit" and "Dim."

If you think those names are strange,
Well, don't blame
Her or him.

At school, the teacher called the roll:
"Bird Brain"
"Dim Wit"
"Lame Brain"
"Nit Wit"

All the other children
Thought it was a hilarious game.
And the moral of the story is...

Be thankful for your name!

Thanksgiving

I ate a lot of turkey
And mashed potatoes too,
A heaping mound of stuffing
And a little bit of stew.

Sweet potatoes and marshmallows
And twenty-seven peas,
Almost all the cranberry sauce,
And a slice of cheese.

Lots and lots of gravy
And tons of apple cider,
Cakes, and pies, and cookies—
My belt was getting tighter!

I could hardly move,
I could hardly talk,
My stomach was so huge,
That I could hardly walk.

I was very, very frightened,
I thought I might explode.
The other kids went out to play
While I rolled down the road.

I ended up three states away,
And boy, was I a mess!
As for next Thanksgiving,
I think I'll eat a little less...

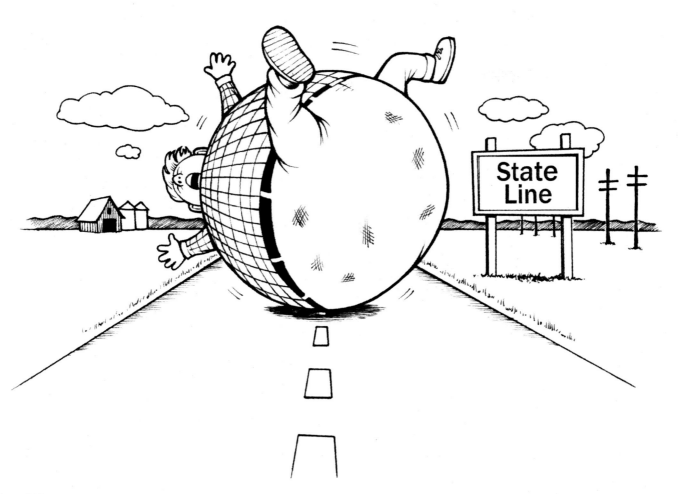

What About Me?

Alycia wanted more, than
Boris who's a bore.
Carlyn said, "Me too,"
Daniella said, "Too few."
Ellen was a brat,
Fred stomped on his hat.

Gracie wasn't nice,
Hank cried at least twice.
Irene sighed,
Johnny lied,
Krista just went numb.

Lauren cursed,
Melanie was worse,
Nicole said, "It's dumb."
Olivia rolled her eyes,
Peter said, "Wrong size."

Quincy huffed,
Richie puffed,
Samantha groaned,
Toni moaned,
Ursula just went nuts.

Vernon screamed,
Wendy schemed,
Xavier was rude,
Yolanda sued,
Zack barfed out his guts.

So if you're unhappy
With what you get,
Instead of being mad,
At least say, "Thank you."
"That's very nice,"
And just pretend you're glad.

Inside Out

I woke up inside out,
And didn't know what to do.

Yes, I woke up inside out,
And I didn't have a clue.

You could see my brains,
But you couldn't see my nose.

You could see my heart,
But you couldn't see my toes.

My skin was on the inside,
But my bones were all exposed.

My appendix, it dangled...
My liver was tangled.
My ears and my eyes were inside,

I couldn't hear and I couldn't see,
I was certain that I must have died.

Then I sneezed so hard that my insides shook,
And everything turned all around.

I was happy just being alive,
And seeing my feet on the ground.

Who's That?

Respect your elders,
Say "please" and "thank you."
And never hit your brother.

Wash your hands,
And wipe your feet,
And always obey your mother.

Eat your spinach,
Say your prayers,
And never forget your chores.

Never yell,
And never cry.
Never slam any doors.

Your mom or dad
May still complain
Instead of jumping for joy.

They'll be confused,
And wonder out loud,
"What happened to our little boy?"

Same Old Same Old

I've watched the
Same old movie
A hundred and
Thirty seven times.

I guess I could
Write poetry, and
Concentrate on rhymes.

But I just want
To watch that movie
Again, and again, and again.

Instead of writing
All about
A big, fat, purple hen.

I know what's
Going to happen.
I've seen it all before.

But I'd still
Rather watch it
Than do something
That's a bore.

So, when you're
Writing poetry,
And thinking it's so great,

I'll be watching
That movie again.
Make it one hundred thirty eight!

If

If I played for the Yankees,
I'd hit five home runs in a game.
If I was the president,
I'd delight in all the fame.

If I was a movie star,
"We love you," my fans would say.
And if I was the principal,
There'd be no school today.

Round & Round

We were playing hide and seek,
And I hid in the hamper.
I put the wet towels over me,
It was getting damper.

My father dumped the hamper stuff
Into the washing machine.
Smelly underwear, sheets and towels,
Me and some old blue jeans.

Powdery detergent
And a half a cup of bleach.
No way could I stop it,
The controls were out of reach.

For thirty minutes
I soaked and spun.
I looked like a prune,
It wasn't much fun.

For thirty minutes
I was busy
With being nauseous
And being dizzy.

It finally stopped,
I yelled, "Whoopee!"
In a minute or two,
I would be free.

But the unexpected did occur,
Really I'm not a liar.
Before I knew what happened,
I was thrown into the dryer.

159 degrees, phew!
Like being in a torture tank.
And did I happen to mention
The six or seven inches that I shrank?

About an hour later
I emerged dry but weak.
Nobody had found me,
I had won "hide and seek."

Smaller than when I started,
And a lot cleaner too,
Next time I'll avoid the hamper
And pick a spot with a better view.

Mr. Black & Mr. White

Mr. White was black
And Mr. Black was white
So if you said "That's Black or White,"
Would you be wrong or right?

White could be Black
Or Black could be White,
It's just not as clear
Like it's day or it's night.

It really doesn't matter
Who's Black and who's White—
So let's not fight...
Alright?

Dear Old Mom

Mom says she needs her morning coffee
To become a human being.
Once I saw her at six in the morning,
And I screamed, "What is that thing?"

One eye was up and one was down.
There was a scowl, there was a frown.
I whispered to my older brother,
"Gee, what happened to our mother?"

Then she had her morning coffee,
And as sure as my name's "Tom,"
Everything began to change
And there was dear, old mom.

The Best Drinkin' Lemonade Stand

We made a glass of lemonade,
And it tasted good.
So we started a lemonade stand
In our neighborhood.

We called it
Best Drinkin' Lemonade Stand,
The best darn lemonade
In all the land.

We were so busy
That we opened one more.
A couple of more,
And then we had four.

Lemonade experts came
From far and from wide.
They wanted our secret,
We had nothing to hide.

It's organic lemons,
Chilled to thirty degrees.
Add a pinch of honey,
And throw in bees' knees.

Put in heaping mounds of sugar,
An eyebrow from an eel,
Add a good amount of love,
And a tad of orange peel.

Mix it in a blender,
Shake and bake and stir.
Make enough for you and me,
And him, and them, and her.

Add crushed ice
And chilled brown rice,
Say, "Abracadabra,"
Not once, but twice.

There's nothing in the world
That's quite as nice.
It's five dollars a glass,
And worth the price.

The lemonade made
At Best Drinkin' Lemonade Stand
Is now available
Throughout all the land.

We have stands in fifty states,
And Guam and Moscow too.
Our lemonade's sold in Africa,
Cape Cod, and the London Zoo.

Millions and millions
Of dollars were made.
They honored us with
The world's biggest parade.

Now we have bracelets
Of diamonds and jade.
We have a butler,
And also a maid.

And it all began
That day we played,
And made one little glass
Of lemonade.

Pockets, Pants & Porcupines

I have a pet porcupine,
I keep him in my pocket.
His quills tear all my pants to shreds,
I think I better stop it.

Cannibal Carl

He'll eat your cheeks,
And bite your thighs.
He'll mash your nose
In cherry pies.

He'll roast your chin,
And boil your hands,
And cook your tonsils
In blood soaked pans.

He'll fry your face,
And bake your brain.
So if you see him,
Take the train...

Or a car, or bus
Or an airplane,
Because your loss
Will be his gain.

It really Happened

A hippopotamus
And a rhinoceros
Got on a school bus.

So there wasn't any room
For me or Sal,
David, Jen, or Gus.

So we had to walk
Five miles to school,
And got there very late.

We told our teacher
What had happened,
And she was quite irate.

She accused us
All of lying,
And making a big fuss.

A hippo and a rhino?
Riding?
On a bus?

She was going
To call our parents.
It gave us quite a scare.

The principal
Came in and said,
"Good afternoon, we have visitors here."

He introduced the hippo, and the rhino
too.
He told us they were visiting
From the San Diego Zoo.

The teacher felt so bad
That she had doubted
Our explanation.

She asked for
Our forgiveness,
For all the aggravation.

So the next time
Me and Sal,
David, Jen, and Gus

Don't get to school on time,
'Cause we missed
That yellow bus,

When the teacher
Raises her brow and
Asks us why we were late,

We'll tell her that
An elephant and
A gorilla made us wait.

Aliens

A spaceship landed
On my roof.
Of course, of this
I have no proof.

I was up at
The crack of dawn,
And saw aliens walking
On my lawn!

By the time you look,
They may be gone.
That doesn't mean I'm lying.

I want to tell
A thrilling story...
Can't you see I'm trying?

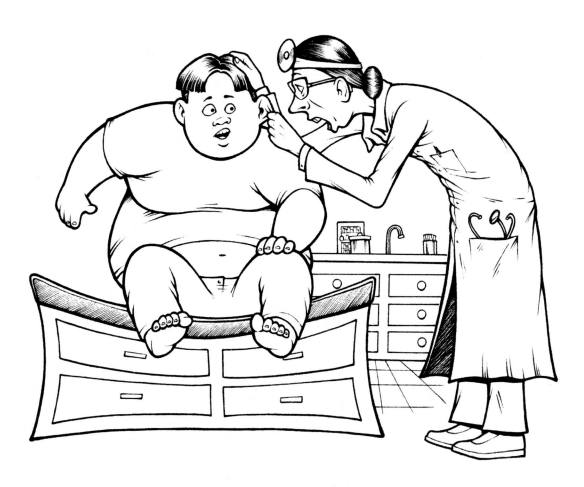

Eat No More Pies

The doctor tugged my ear
And said, "Stick out your tongue, my dear."

She pressed on my nose,
And stepped on my toes,

Shined a light in my eyes,
Pinched both my thighs,

Remarked on my size,
Said, "Eat no more pies,

Wear only bow ties,"
Then said her good-byes.

(And I didn't even get a lollipop.)

Humpty at the Mall

Humpty Dumpty sat high on a wall
At the entrance of a huge mall.

He wouldn't stand up,
He'd only sit down.
From on top of the wall
He could see the whole town.

He was thirsty and tired, with nothing to eat.
His back, it was aching. He had icy cold feet.

He hadn't slept
In forty-three days,
Just sitting, and sitting
With a fixed gaze.

He hoped to be rescued,
He hoped to be saved.
He was such a good egg,
So well behaved.

So Humpty Dumpty
Sat at the mall,
And poor, frightened Humpty
Had a great fall.

Nancy and Scotty,
Caitlyn and Ken,
Couldn't put Humpty
Together again.

Next to the pile
Of his arms and his legs,
Four boys were feasting
On scrambled eggs.

After hours and hours,
They felt so much pain,
They threw it all up.
It had been in vain.

Those boys-
Sammy and Carl,
And Tony and Ben,
Never, NEVER ate eggs again!

Ernest

When Ernest was four years old,
He walked into a store
That sold noses and said,
"I'll take that one."

And that's the story
About the first time
Ernest ever picked his nose.

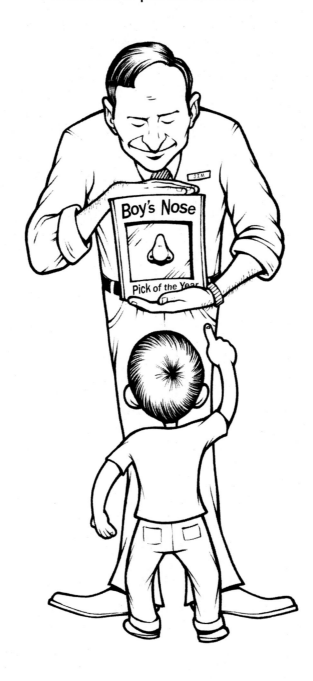

Someday

I live in the city,
And my name is "Dave."
I've never seen the ocean,
And I never rode a wave.

Let me explain further,
Let me be more specific.
When it comes to oceans,
I don't know "Atlantic" from "Pacific."

I've never used a "boogie board,"
I've never seen the surf.
My feet have never gotten wet,
They've always been on turf.

When I grow up,
I'll find a beach,
And I'll ride every wave.

And far and wide,
Wherever I go,
They'll call me "Surfer Dave."

A Dollar A Bunch

Get some arms, or legs, or feet,
They're two for a buck, ninety-five.
Take a walk down the aisle of chests,
A good one might keep you alive.

They've got chins and wrists
For a nickel a piece.
The elbows are plenty,
And come with some grease.

Eyes are a quarter,
Knees are a dime.
Get a ten pack of fingers,
And you will save time.

It's an enormous supermarket
That sells body parts,
In case you need jaws,
Or in case you need hearts.

Yesterday, I bought
Some lips and some thighs.
Today, I returned them,
They were the wrong size.

Instead of fruit and vegetables,
They sell legs and hands.
You can even buy a dozen ears,
They come in aluminum cans.

Eyebrows are a penny each,
I bought a hundred and fifty.
My mother made an eyebrow scarf,
It's really kind of nifty.

Necks are on special today,
A dollar will get you a bunch.
I'm going to spend all my money,
Then go home and have a big lunch.

People are stopping and staring at me,
Like I'm a Tyrannosaurus Rex.
I guess they've never seen a boy
With twenty-seven necks.

When my family looked at me,
They thought I was insane.
They said, "Go right back to the store
And buy yourself a brain!"

Lost & Found

Thanks for helping me look...
Yes, I lost it down the street.
I know that we can find it,
If we get on our hands and feet.

Please keep looking with me,
We have to look some more.
Oh yes, I guess it would help
If you knew what we're looking for.

Well, it's a thingamujig, a doodad,
It's difficult to explain.
I hope you don't mind crawling around
In this horrendous, heavy rain.

You're still not sure what we're looking for?
Well, let me try again.
It's a doojiggy, a gizmo, a thingamabob,
And I lost it way back when.

How to describe it exactly,
It's difficult to know.
I hope you don't mind crawling around
In this cold, colossal snow.

Just look for a whatchamacallit,
A doohicky, a fandangle.
I'm sure that, by tomorrow,
We'll have covered every angle.

Oops, I suddenly remembered something
That I definitely should say.
Thanks a lot for helping me look,
But I found it yesterday!

It's Not My Fault
(He Should Have Been Wearing Earmuffs)

I threw a snowball in the air,
Where it landed
I know not where.

But then I saw
A grizzly bear
With a snowball in his ear.

He looked at me
With a sneer
And a growl.

It felt like
I had to move
My bowel.

I ran all day,
And I ran all night,
'Til that bear was out of sight.

So, if you throw
A snowball in the air...
Try not to hit a grizzly bear.

Flat as a Silver Dollar Pancake

Peter Paul
Was one inch tall,
Or maybe we should say,
He was one inch small.

A friend threw him
A basketball,
And that was the end
Of Peter Paul.

Dead on the Living Room Floor

Nothin' to do,
So I'm gonna play dead.
Make wounds on my body,
And wounds on my head.

Marinara sauce and ketchup,
I mixed up for blood,
And poured it all over me
Like a flood of mud.

It looked like I'd been shot
From my head to my toe.
No one's ever looked more dead,
Not even on a TV show.

Waiting to be discovered,
Laying dead on the living room floor,
Finally I heard someone coming,
Walking through the front door.

I didn't move a muscle,
I didn't make a sound.
I didn't even dare to breathe,
I wasn't fooling around.

I guessed that any minute
An ambulance would come,
And carry me out on a stretcher
Past my crying dad or mom.

It must have been quite shocking,
I looked so dead and gooky.
So imagine my surprise when Mom said...
"Hi Kevin, would you like a cookie?"

Rainy Day

It's rainy and I'm tired...
All I want to do is sleep,
Curl up with the blankets
And not hear a peep.

But the cat is walking
On my head
And the hamster's crawling
In the bed.

Horns are blasting
Beep Beep Beep!
Can't I just go
Back to sleep?

It's rainy and I'm tired...
All I want to do is sleep,
Curl up with the blankets
And not hear a peep peep peep.

But the phone is ringing
Off the hook
Or is it part of a dream?

I just rolled over
On a book
And a donut filled with cream.

It's rainy and I'm tired...
And all I want to do is sleep,
Curl up with the blankets
And not hear a peep.

But my baby sister is crying
And an alarm is going off.
I just want to go to sleep
This pillow is so soft.

I guess it's just not meant to be...
OK, I'll get up soon.
I'm sure I could have slept some more,
What's that? Oh! It's three in the afternoon?!

My Refrigerator

My refrigerator
Talks to me.
It says, "Come open my door."

It says, "Wouldn't you like
Some ice cream?"
And, "How would you like some more?"

Me

Justin is skinny,
George is fat.
This is this,
And that is that.

She is big,
He is little.
A flute makes music,
But is not a fiddle.

He has a face,
But it's not like mine.
It's very different,
But that's just fine.

Because if everyone
Looked just like me,
I'm not sure
Who I would be!

A Van of Sardines
(Or a Can of Kids)

Sixteen kids squeezed
Into a van...
Packed so tight
Like sardines in a can.

Stephanie, Nicholas, Paul, Denzel,
Haley, Jeff, and Nan.
Matthew, Kaitlyn, Sofia, Owen,
Madison, three Ryans, and a Dan.

Every inch was taken,
You could hardly move at all.
And then, we all heard the fart,
It was either Dan or Paul.

It smelled like gads of rotten eggs,
Mixed with barf and stinky goop.
No one could open a window,
We were not a happy group.

So, next time you consider
Putting sixteen kids in a van,
Open all the windows,
Bring air fresheners and a fan.

And never, ever, ever,
Invite Paul or invite Dan.

If Only...

If only I was taller.
If only my nose was smaller.
If only I was strong.
If only I would never be wrong.

If only I had a pony.
If only we had a pool.
If only I wasn't so bony.
If only I didn't have school.

If only everyone liked me.
If only I could just play.
If only the world was like that,
Oh, how I would love everyday.

Ugly Green Thing

There's an ugly, green thing
With seventeen legs
Crawling on your back.

It's got three horns,
Is chewing gum,
And carrying a sack.

It has a gigantic
Orange tongue, and
A very hairy nose.

It's going toward your stomach,
And eating through
Your clothes.

I know you think I'm lying,
And that I want to make you look...
But please believe me, please!
That ugly thing's a crook.

It just took your belly button,
And put it in its sack.
I guess you're pretty lucky,
'Cause it didn't take your back.

Chewing Away

Billy blew the biggest bubbles
Of all the boys in town.
He chewed his bubble gum all the time,
More than anyone around.

In spite of many warnings
From his dear old mother,
He would stuff gum in his mouth,
One piece after another.

And on, and on it went,
So by the end of every day,
With zillions of pieces of bubble gum,
Billy was chewing away.

One windy day
In early fall,
Billy blew the most humongous
Bubble of them all.

So pink and round,
Like a huge balloon.
The wind took him and his bubble
Up toward the moon...

So when you look
Up to the skies,
And you see something
That astounds your eyes,

If it's not a plane,
Or Superman,
Or a spaceship from Mars
That's about to land,

Don't get scared or scream,
Don't get in trouble,
It's only Billy
And his zillion piece bubble.

Were There Only Seven?

Can you name the seven dwarves?
I'm pretty sure I can.
There was "Bumpy,"
"Lumpy," "Frumpy," and "Dumpy,"
"Plumpy," "Stumpy," and "Jumpy."

Wow, I knew them all!
Don't I deserve a bow?
If you know any other dwarves,
You can say them now.

(Go ahead, I mean it!)

Chicken Walk

Why did the chicken
Walk across the road?

Was it to get to the other side?

Nope.
The chicken walked across the road
Because he couldn't get a ride!

Author Author Author

The chef wrote a book,
It was called a cookbook.

The thief wrote a book,
It was called a crookbook.

The nerd wrote a book,
It was called a schnookbook.

The cook baked the crook's book,
The crook stole the schnook's book,

The schnook was left without a book.
Well, what can you expect from a schnook?

(And he cried, "Wee wee wee," all the way home.)

The Spider

In a corner of my room
Where the wall and ceiling meet,
A spider web is shimmering
In the blistering heat.

There was a spider in it yesterday,
But he's not in sight today.
I hope that no one stepped on him,
I hope that he's OK.

Confusion

My mother asked me
If I wanted an ear of corn
As I sat by the foot of the bed.

It was all quite confusing!
What a picture I had
Inside my head!

My Invention

I just built
A thigamujig
With a gear
And a zig and a
Zag and a rig

It's not very big
It will dig
Like a pig
With its cam
And its clerf
And its frig
And its glig

What an invention!
My thigamujig.

Too Bad it Had to End Like This

He called me a "wimp"
So I called him a "blimp"

He said I was "crazy"
I told him he's "lazy"

He yelled "You're scared!"
I shouted "You're weird!"

He called me a "nerd"
I called him a "turd"

He called me a "jerk"
And I couldn't think of anything
To call him that rhymed with "jerk"...

So that's the end of this poem.

The Snail

They said I was fast as a snail.
I never knew that snails were fast.
If I was as fast as a snail,
Then why did I finish last?

A Good Story

Good Morning!
Good Afternoon,
Good Night...
Good Bye!

A Bad Story

This stinks!
Hissssssssssss,
Peeee Ew,
Terrible,
Ugh,
BOO!

The End.

The Thief

A caterpillar crawled
Into my ear
And got inside my head.

As spiders scampered
Up my nose
I was sure that I'd be dead.

A giant beetle
Got into my mouth
And slithered down my throat.

And on the way
He stole my pen
So nothing more I wrote.

The End